the most Terrible of all

by
Muon Thị Văn

monsters by
Matt Myers

Margaret K. McElderry Books
New York · London · Toronto · Sydney · New Delhi

For Selah —M. T. V.

For all the little monsters
at Chantilly Montessori elementary —M. M.

MARGARET K. McELDERRY BOOKS

An imprint of Simon & Schuster Children's Publishing Division

1230 Avenue of the Americas, New York, New York 10020

Text copyright © 2019 by Muon Van · Illustrations copyright © 2019 by Matt Myers

For information about special discounts for bulk purchases, please contact Simon & Schuster Special
Sales at 1-866-506-1949 or business@simonandschuster.com.

The Simon & Schuster Speakers Bureau can bring authors to your live event. For more information or
to book an event, contact the Simon & Schuster Speakers Bureau at 1-866-248-3049
or visit our website at www.simonspeakers.com.

Book design by Semadar Megged · The text for this book was set in Mr Dodo Light.

The illustrations for this book were painted in acrylic and oil. · Manufactured in China · 0119 SCP

First Edition

2 4 6 8 10 9 7 5 3 1

Library of Congress Cataloging-in-Publication Data

Names: Van, Muon, author. | Myers, Matt, illustrator.

Title: The most terrible of all / by Muon Thi Van : monsters by Matt Myers.

Description: First edition. | New York : Margaret K. McElderry Books, 2019. | Summary: When a monster
meets his neighbor's new baby he discovers true terribleness can come in tiny packages.

Identifiers: LCCN 2018026425 (print) | LCCN 2018029592 (eBook)

ISBN 9781534417175 (eBook) | ISBN 9781534417168 (hardback)

Subjects: | CYAC: Monsters—Fiction. | Babies—Fiction. | Humorous stories. | BISAC: JUVENILE FICTION /
Humorous Stories. | JUVENILE FICTION / Family / New Baby. | JUVENILE FICTION / Monsters.

Classification: LCC PZ7.1.V35 (eBook) | LCC PZ7.1.V35 Mo 2019 (print) | DDC [E]—dc23

LC record available at https://lccn.loc.gov/2018026425

his is Smugg.
He is the most terrible monster ever.
Even his magic mirror says so.

Every morning, right after he slimes himself
with twenty frogs, he asks,
"Mirror, mirror, on the wall,
who's the most terrible one of all?"

The mirror always replies,
"Ugly Smuggly, my smelly wuggly,
you are the most terrible one of all."

"Truly?"

"True as the slime and grime dripping from your nose.
True as the snails and tails creeping between your toes."

But this morning, something was different.
"Mirror, mirror, on the wall, who's the most terrible one of all?"

"Ugly Smuggly, my foaming nuggly,
you are pretty terrible, it's true. But . . .

"another has arrived next door, another who's a million times more terrible than you."

"Another who's a million times more terrible than me? Who is it? How can that be?"

Smugg sharpened his claws. "I'll show you who's the most terrible one of all."

Smugg stomped out of the
house, trampled the frogs,
broke the fence, squashed
the flowers, and pushed
down the neighbor's door.

Smugg had never seen so many
wild beasts before.

He pulled down a beast
swinging from the chandelier.
"Are you the one who's the most
terrible of all?"

"No, not me! Fang is the most terrible!
She's under there!"

"Are you the one who's the most terrible of all?"

"No, not me! Jaws and Claws are the most terrible! They're over there!"

"Are you the one who's the most terrible of all?"
"No, not me!" said Claws.
Jaws shook his head.

Just then a thundering noise
rattled the windows and doors.
"What was that?" whispered Smugg.
"Oh, that's our new sister," said Claws.
"She's upstairs and she's really
the most terrible of all!"

"I can be more terrible than that!" said Smugg.
He howled and growled as he stomped up the stairs.

The little beast didn't look so terrible.

He leaned in close.
The little beast pulled his hair.
"I told you she was terrible," said Claws.

"I can be more terrible than that!"

said Smugg.

He took a huge bite out of the crib.

But the little beast was just getting started.

She wrote on the walls.

She teased the pets.

She ripped the books.

And she said her first word.
(It was not a nice one.)

Oh, and she spilled some water, too.

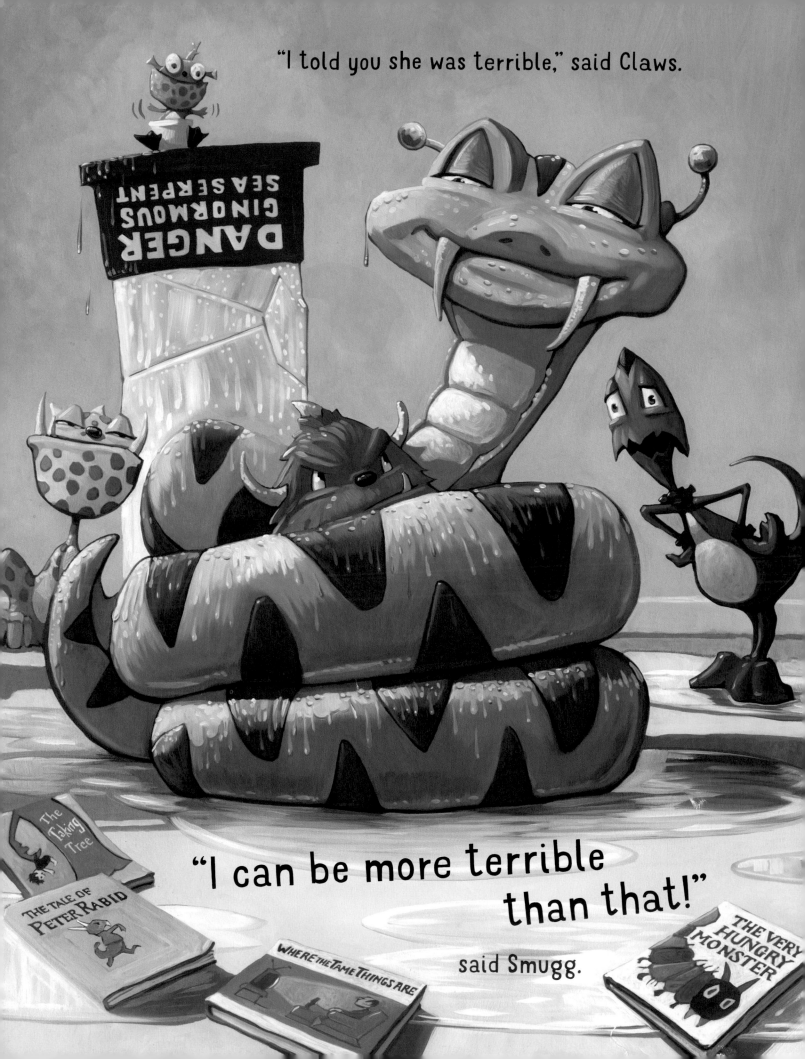

He grabbed the serpent by the tail.

He rolled it up.

He kicked it.

The little beast started crying.

Smugg picked up the little beast.

She stopped crying . . .

and bit his nose.

He tried shaking her off,
but he only got dizzy.

He crashed into the wall.
She still held on.

He fell straight out the window and . . .

Smugg couldn't believe it.
The little beast was still on his head.
The other beasts ran
out of the house.

"I told you she was
terrible," said Claws.

Suddenly, there was a big, stinky gust of wind.

"I think someone needs a diaper change,"
said Jaws, holding his nose.
The little beast squeezed Smugg
even tighter.

"I think the baby likes you," said Fang.

Smugg glowered at the baby.
The baby grinned at Smugg.
"I dont like anyone," said Smugg.
"We'll see about her."

Smugg stomped across the lawn, squashed the flowers, kicked the fence, trampled the frogs, and pushed down his door.

"Mirror, mirror, on the wall,
who's the most terrible one of all. . . .

"The most terrible over two feet tall?"